W9-AJP-883

Ear

NEW MEXICO

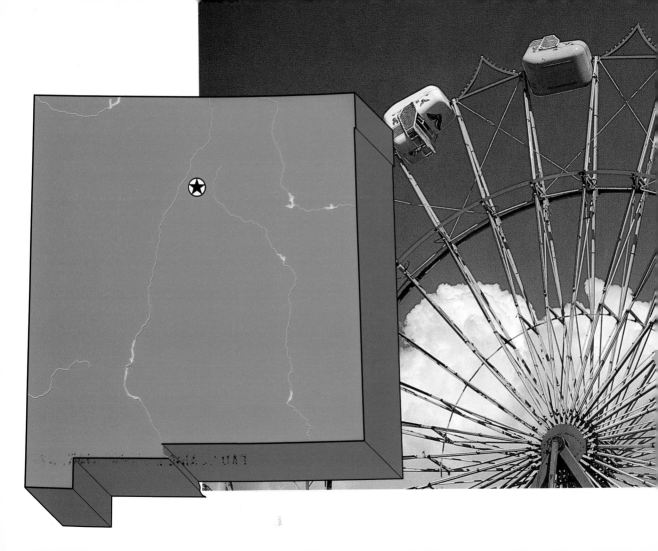

NEW MEXICO

Theresa S. Early

EAU CLAIRE DISTRICT LIBRARY

Lerner Publications Company

T 111456

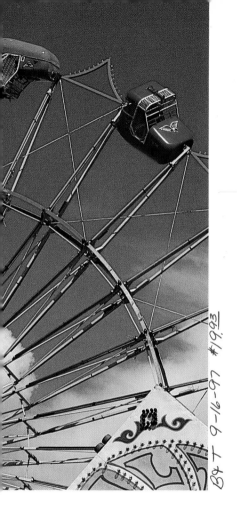

Copyright © 1993 by Lerner Publications Company, Minneapolis, Minnesota

All rights reserved. International copyright secured. No part of this book may be reproduced, stored in a retrieval system, or transmitted in any form or by any means—electronic, mechanical, photocopying, recording, or otherwise—without the prior written permission of Lerner Publications Company, except for the inclusion of brief quotations in an acknowledged review.

LIBRARY OF CONGRESS
CATALOGING-IN-PUBLICATION DATA
Early, Theresa S.
    New Mexico / Theresa S. Early.
        p.   cm. — (Hello USA)
    Includes index.
    Summary: Introduces the geography, history, people, industries, and other highlights of New Mexico.
    ISBN 0-8225-2748-0 (lib. bdg.)
    1. New Mexico—Juvenile literature.
[1. New Mexico.] I. Title. II. Series.
F796.3.E18   1992
978.9—dc20   92-13364
                                             CIP
                                              AC

Cover photograph by Kent & Donna Dannen.

The glossary that begins on page 68 gives definitions of words shown in **bold type** in the text.

Manufactured in the United States of America

1 2 3 4 5 6 98 97 96 95 94 93

 This book is printed on acid-free, recyclable paper.

CONTENTS

Did You Know . . . ?

☐ In 1950 fire fighters rescued a black-bear cub from a fire in New Mexico's Lincoln National Forest. They called the cub Smokey Bear and made him the symbol of the U.S. Forest Service's effort to prevent forest fires.

☐ Founded in 1610, Santa Fe, New Mexico, is the oldest capital city in the United States.

After being rescued, Smokey Bear received visitors at the National Zoological Park in Washington, D.C.

6

The world's first atomic bomb was tested in New Mexico at Trinity Site, near Alamogordo, on July 16, 1945.

In addition to English, most New Mexicans speak at least one other language. Spanish is the second most common language, followed by American Indian tongues including Apache, Navajo, and various Pueblo languages.

At its northwestern corner, New Mexico touches Arizona, Utah, and Colorado. This point is the only place in the United States where four states meet.

A sandhill crane *(above)* flies over the Bosque del Apache National Wildlife Refuge in central New Mexico. Rock formations *(right)* are only part of the unique landscape found at Angel Peak National Recreation Area in northwestern New Mexico.

A Trip
Around the State

Of the 50 states, New Mexico is the fifth largest in area. It offers miles and miles of unending beauty, from forested mountains to colorful deserts and vast plains. Because of its breathtaking scenery, New Mexico is often called the Land of Enchantment.

New Mexico lies in the heart of the Southwest. The state is bordered on the west by Arizona, to the northwest by Utah, on the north by Colorado, and on the east by Texas and Oklahoma. Texas and the country of Mexico mark New Mexico's southern border.

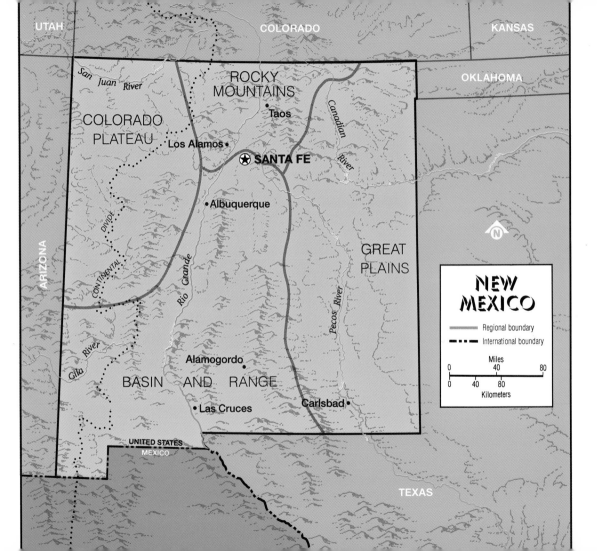

UTAH

COLORADO

KANSAS

OKLAHOMA

San Juan River

ROCKY
MOUNTAINS

Canadian River

COLORADO
PLATEAU

• Taos

• Los Alamos

⊛ SANTA FE

ARIZONA

CONTINENTAL DIVIDE

• Albuquerque

Rio Grande

GREAT
PLAINS

N

Gila River

Pecos River

BASIN   AND   RANGE

• Alamogordo

• Las Cruces

• Carlsbad

UNITED STATES
MEXICO

TEXAS

NEW MEXICO

Regional boundary
International boundary

Miles
0   40   80

0   40   80
Kilometers

New Mexico is divided into four regions—the Rocky Mountains, the Colorado Plateau, the Basin and Range, and the Great Plains. The first three regions have mountains, but all of the state is higher—and much of it is drier—than most other places in the United States.

The Rocky Mountain region in north central New Mexico is named after the chain of mountains that stretches across it. Reaching from Alaska to New Mexico, the Rocky Mountains (also called the Rockies) form the longest mountain system in North America.

The cholla cactus, which produces bright flowers, grows in New Mexico's Basin and Range region.

The Rockies were formed millions of years ago by volcanoes that spewed layers of hot liquid rock called **lava**. The lava cooled and hardened into mountains. Wind and water gradually wore them down to their present shape.

The Rocky Mountains tower over north central New Mexico.

The Rockies also form much of North America's Continental Divide—a ridge of high land separating the rivers that flow east from those that flow west. In New Mexico, the divide runs through a short stretch of the Rocky Mountains, then through the Colorado Plateau and the Basin and Range.

The Colorado Plateau in northwestern New Mexico is a rocky region made up of mountains and **plateaus,** or flat highlands. Rivers have cut deep canyons and strange,

CLAIRE DISTRICT LIBRARY

beautiful rock sculptures into the plateau. Isolated flat-topped hills, called **mesas**, dot the land.

The Basin and Range region covers much of southern and central New Mexico. Some of the mountain ranges in the region rise more than 10,000 feet (3,048 meters). In between the ranges lie broad valleys, or **basins**, that are so dry they are considered **deserts**. Most of New Mexico's people live in or near the Basin and Range in the Rio Grande Valley. Farms in the valley yield crops such as chili peppers, cotton, and pecans.

White Sands National Monument, which lies in New Mexico's Basin and Range region, is a desert of brilliant white sand.

EAU CLAIRE DISTRICT LIBRARY

The Great Plains region covers the eastern third of the state. The region is wide and nearly flat, although it has deep valleys and mesas in the north. Most of the state's cattle are raised on the Great Plains.

Few rivers flow year-round in New Mexico. Heat and lack of rain cause many of them to dry up during the summer. The state's longest and most important river is the Rio Grande, which flows south across the entire state.

Other chief rivers include the Pecos, Canadian, Gila, and San

Juan. The Pecos and Canadian rivers, as well as the Rio Grande, flow on the east side of the Continental Divide, and the Gila and San Juan rivers flow on the west side.

New Mexico's elevation, or height above sea level, ranges from about 3,000 to 13,000 feet (914 to 3,962 m). Areas at high elevations are colder than areas at low elevations, so the state's climate varies greatly.

In the low southwestern deserts, summer temperatures can be more than 100° F (38° C), and winter temperatures hover around 40° F (4° C). Snow falls almost everywhere in New Mexico, but the low, dry parts of the state receive only about 2 inches (5 centimeters) per year. Rainfall is scarce throughout most of the state.

The Rio Grande, one of the longest rivers in North America, means "big river" in Spanish.

15

In the northern mountains, summer temperatures are cooler than in the south, averaging just below 70° F (21° C). Winter temperatures in the north can be bitterly cold but average about 24° F (–4° C). On the slopes above the northern resort town of Taos, skiers expect a lot of powdery snow—more than 300 inches (762 cm) a year.

Because the weather conditions vary throughout New Mexico, the state contains a wide range of plants and animals. Cactuses and shrubs—such as prickly pear, cholla, and mesquite—thrive in the desert. Horned toads, rattlesnakes, and poisonous spiders—including the tarantula and the black widow —also do well in the desert heat.

A boy learns the joy of fishing for black bass, catfish, perch, and trout in New Mexico.

The sure-footed bighorn sheep *(left)* treads the heights of the Rockies with ease. The bloom of the prickly pear cactus *(below)* is New Mexico's state flower.

In the mountains, piñon trees and alpine fungi grow. Marmots and pikas, two kinds of small furry mammals, frolic at the state's highest elevations. Bighorn sheep and elk climb a bit lower. On the Great Plains and lower mountains, pronghorn antelope and mule deer play.

17

New Mexico's Story

The first people known to live in North America were hunters who probably left Asia at least 12,000 years ago. Eventually, these ancestors of modern-day Native Americans spread throughout North and South America.

Among the first peoples to build permanent villages and farms in the Southwest were the Mogollon and the Anasazi. *Anasazi* is a Navajo Indian word meaning "ancient ones." The early Anasazi are also called the Basket Makers because they were so skillful at weaving baskets. The Anasazi grew corn and beans and trained dogs for hunting. The Indians also made pottery.

Using stone or sun-dried mud, the Anasazi built villages in what is now northwestern New Mexico. Each village was made up of one large building that was several stories high, like an apartment house. The Anasazi left their villages in the late 1200s after a long **drought,** or dry spell, made farming impossible. They moved to other places in what is now New Mexico.

Remains of Pueblo Bonito still stand in Chaco Canyon National Historic Park. The Anasazi village was once five stories high and had more than 1,000 rooms.

Shiprock, a large landform in northwestern New Mexico, is sacred to the Navajo Indians.

Nomadic, or traveling, tribes of Navajo and of Apache Indians eventually moved to the Southwest. The Navajo lived in small family groups. Their homes, called hogans, were built from logs and earth. The Apache traveled in large groups. They lived in tepees made of animal hides or in grass dwellings called wickiups.

By the early 1500s, American Indians lived throughout what is now New Mexico. At the same time, Spain was conquering Indian villages to the south, in what is now Mexico. The Spaniards took a fortune in gold and jewels from the Indians. Eager to find more wealth, the king of Spain set up a Spanish **colony,** or settlement, in Mexico.

Francisco Vásquez de Coronado, a Spanish governor in Mexico, led the first major European expedition to the area that would become New Mexico. In 1540 the group began a long journey in search of more gold. Coronado was looking for the Seven Cities of Cibola— seven cities rich in gold that were rumored to lie north of Mexico.

Coronado and his troops spent two years searching for the Seven Cities of Cibola.

Instead of gold, Coronado found descendants of the Anasazi living in multi-storied villages. The explorers were impressed by the design of the villages, which they called *pueblos* (the Spanish word for "towns"). The Spaniards also named the people who lived in these villages Pueblos.

By 1542 Coronado and his expedition had returned to Mexico to report their failure. Although no

In the 1500s, Spanish explorers met the Indians living in Taos Pueblo. Pueblo Indians still occupy the ancient structure. In fact, it's the only building in the United States that has been continuously inhabited since the 1200s.

gold had been found, rumors still flew that the area just north of Mexico was full of riches—it was a "new" Mexico. New Mexico is what the area has been called ever since.

In 1610 Pedro de Peralta, a Spanish official, established the first permanent Spanish settlement in New Mexico. This settlement, Santa Fe, served as the capital of the colony of New Mexico.

Since earlier attempts to find gold in New Mexico had been fruitless, the goal of the colonists changed. They now intended to preach the official religion of Spain—Catholicism. To turn the Pueblo Indians into Catholics, the Spaniards outlawed Indian religions.

In addition, the Spaniards collected food from the Indians as a tax and forced them to farm land the Spaniards had taken. To make matters worse, smallpox, measles, and other European diseases swept through the villages. One out of every ten Pueblo Indians died of smallpox in 1640.

Shortly after they arrived, Spanish settlers began building churches in the colony of New Mexico.

23

The Pueblo Revolt of 1680

During the 1600s, the Spaniards tried to make the Pueblo Indians dress European and speak Spanish. They also tried to stamp out the Pueblo religions, replacing them with a very different faith—Catholicism. Catholics worshipped one god, while the Pueblos worshipped several spirits. Some Pueblos accepted the Catholic religion, or parts of it. A Pueblo Indian artist, for example, painted the Madonna *(right)* with Pueblo Indian features. But others rejected Catholicism entirely.

Popé, an Indian religious leader from San Juan Pueblo, encouraged Indians to remain true to their religion. In 1675 Spanish soldiers arrested 47 Pueblo religious leaders —including Popé. The Spaniards hanged three of the men and whipped and jailed most of the others. After Popé was released from jail, he helped plan a rebellion.

On August 10, 1680, Pueblo Indians throughout the colony of New Mexico attacked Spanish villages, killing more than

400 Spaniards and running the rest out of New Mexico. The Pueblo Revolt of 1680 marked Spain's first loss of an entire colony. Spain reconquered New Mexico in 1693, prompting many Pueblos to leave the area. But those who stayed refused to live under the old Spanish rules. Today, Pueblo religions, as well as culture, are still alive.

Nomadic tribes stole many goods, including pottery, from the more peaceful Pueblo Indians.

The nomadic Apache and Navajo were not as easily overcome. On horses stolen from the Spaniards, the nomads raided both Spanish and Pueblo villages to get items they did not make or raise themselves. They stole food, animals, and blankets.

Overall, the colony of New Mexico was poor. Supplies were sent from Mexico City (the capital of Mexico) only once or twice a year. This was partly because travelers had to cross the Jornada del Muerto, or Journey of Death—90 miles (145 kilometers) of trail with no water. Yet New Mexicans were not allowed to buy or sell goods from anywhere else. They raised or made almost everything they needed. But some items, such as iron pots and sugar, were very scarce.

In the early 1700s, Comanche Indians moved into New Mexico from the northwest. Their raids on the Spaniards and the Pueblos were fierce. Sometimes the Comanche were joined by Ute Indians from the north. By the 1740s, the Comanche had taken control of much of eastern New Mexico.

About 30 years later, the Spaniards and the Pueblo Indians joined forces in a successful battle against the Comanche. By 1786 the New Mexican and the Coman-

che leaders had signed a peace **treaty,** an agreement to end the warfare.

In 1821 Mexico gained independence from Spain. New Mexicans were now governed by Mexican leaders, not by the king of Spain. New Mexicans celebrated because Mexico granted them new freedoms, including the right to trade with outsiders.

William Becknell, a trader from Missouri, heard of Mexico's independence and headed for New Mexico. He was the first trader from the United States to reach Santa Fe. Becknell found New Mexicans eager for the goods he offered and willing to pay any price for them.

Trade between the United States and New Mexico flourished. Traders drove covered wagons along a well-marked route called the Santa Fe Trail, which ran from Independence, Missouri, to Santa Fe. Santa Fe began to grow. New settlers came to town selling hats, gloves, silverware, books, spices, medicine, and paint to eager customers. **Anglos,** as these settlers from the United States were called, also built stores and banks.

The Comanche Indians *(facing page)* were expert horseback riders.

During the 1800s, weary traders and settlers were relieved to finally reach Santa Fe after a long journey on the Santa Fe Trail.

As more U.S. citizens moved southwest, the U.S. government became interested in New Mexico and other Mexican territories. When Mexico refused to sell its territories to the United States, the two countries began fighting in what became known as the Mexican War (1846–1848).

In 1846 U.S. troops arrived in Santa Fe prepared for battle. But the New Mexican governor, fearing defeat, had already dismissed his troops and fled south. In other Mexican territories, battles continued until 1848, when the war officially ended. As a result of its victory, the United States got most of the Southwest, including New Mexico.

In 1850 the U.S. government established boundaries for the Territory of New Mexico. It included what are now New Mexico and Arizona and parts of Colorado and Nevada. In 1853 the United States paid Mexico for more land at the southern edge of the territory. This deal was known as the Gadsden Purchase.

U.S. general Stephen Kearny claimed New Mexico for his country in 1846 during the Mexican War.

As a U.S. territory, New Mexico began to change. The U.S. government offered free farmland to new settlers, attracting many Anglos to the area. Others came to make money in trade. The Spaniards and Pueblo lost much of their land to Anglo settlers. Spaniards and Pueblos are still struggling to regain this land.

Some of the Anglos came from Southern states, where slavery was allowed. In 1861 the Civil War broke out between the Southern states and the Northern states, which wanted to end slavery. The Territory of New Mexico officially sided with the North, or the Union. But a lot of U.S. Army officers in New Mexico sided with the South, or the Confederacy. Many of these officers resigned from the U.S. Army so that they could join Confederate forces.

The Confederates quickly captured much of New Mexico, including Santa Fe and the growing city of Albuquerque. The Union army recaptured New Mexico after defeating the Confederates at the Battle of Glorieta Pass in 1862. The Union victory kept the Confederates from controlling the Southwest and California.

While army troops were busy fighting the Civil War, the Apache and Navajo increased their raiding. But by 1863, U.S. troops had defeated the Indians and sent them to a **reservation**—an area of land for Indians to live on. Life on Bosque Redondo Reservation in eastern New Mexico was extremely difficult. The land was too poor

Many Indians died while being taken across the rough country that led to Bosque Redondo Reservation. The difficult journey became known to the Navajo as the Long Walk. When they arrived at the reservation, the survivors were closely guarded by U.S. soldiers.

and dry to farm, and the Indians could not raise enough food for themselves. Thousands died.

Eventually, the Apache simply left the reservation. Some went back to their homeland in south central New Mexico. The U.S. government allowed them to stay and simply created another reservation there. Other Apache were settled on a reservation in northern New Mexico. The Navajo were also allowed to return to their own lands.

Meanwhile traders and ranchers were busy in New Mexico. The territory's grasslands were excellent for grazing sheep, which had become a big money-maker for New Mexico's farmers. After the Civil War, corn, wheat, and cattle

The Apache were able to grow healthy crops on their new reservation in northern New Mexico.

gained in importance. Soon, trails crisscrossed the state as ranchers drove cattle from their grazing ranges to the nearest market.

As mining *(bottom far right)* **increased in New Mexico, trains** *(right)* **were needed to ship metal ore to the States. Soon after trains began arriving in Albuquerque, the bustling city was hosting a popular balloon festival** *(top far right).*

Silver and gold mining had become important in southwestern New Mexico by the 1870s. Towns grew up overnight where ore was found. But as soon as the ore was gone, the miners moved away, leaving only ghost towns.

In 1878 train tracks were laid across New Mexico. Cattle, sheep, and metal ore could now be shipped to market on trains. Albuquerque became the railroad and business center of New Mexico.

34

Legends from a Lawless Land

When people think of the Wild West, they often picture scenes from old western movies. New Mexico of the late 1800s was more than the harmless loud saloons and gambling halls on the silver screen—it was the real Wild West. Few laws —and even fewer law enforcers—existed in the territory. Feuds broke out over almost anything, and the result was sometimes deadly.

Some feuds turned into wars. During the 1870s, for example, ranchers in Lincoln County, New Mexico, fought over land and over who would supply cattle to the U.S. Army, which paid high prices for beef. During

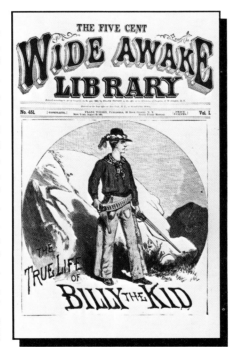

what became known as the Lincoln County War, ranchers hired gunhands to threaten or kill competing ranchers. Cattle baron John Tunstall hired a young gunslinger named William H. Bonney, better known as Billy the Kid.

When Tunstall was shot dead in 1878 by an enemy, Billy the Kid declared he would kill anyone involved in the shooting. Bloody feuds followed, and U.S. Army troops were brought in to restore order. But the Lincoln County War did not officially end until Sheriff Pat Garrett shot and killed Billy the Kid near Fort Sumner, New Mexico, in 1881.

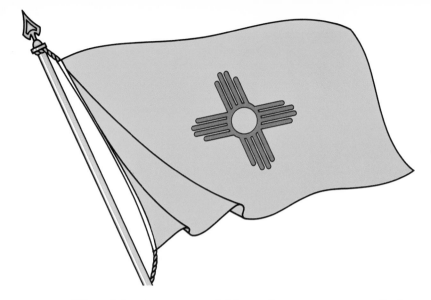

The red design on New Mexico's flag stands for the sun, a symbol of the Zia band of Pueblo Indians. The flag's colors are similar to those of the Spanish flag, reminding New Mexicans of their colonial history.

New Mexico seemed like a foreign place to many Americans. Most New Mexicans spoke Spanish. Nevertheless, on January 6, 1912, New Mexico became the 47th state.

During the Great Depression, the long economic slump of the 1930s, jobs were hard to find. To make matters worse, drought ravaged the state. Some areas were so dry from lack of rain that the wind whipped up the loose soil and blew black clouds of dust across the land. Crops failed and animals died. These areas were part of the **Dust Bowl,** the name given to a section of the United States that suffered from droughts.

37

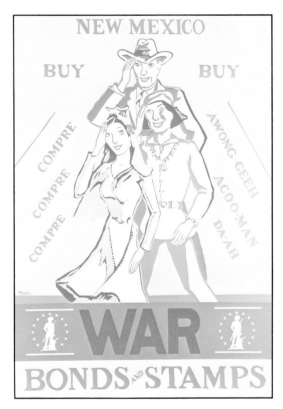

A World War II poster for New Mexicans was printed in English, Spanish, and several Indian languages.

The outbreak of World War II in 1939 brought better economic times to New Mexico. In 1942 J. Robert Oppenheimer, a scientist, chose Los Alamos Ranch School outside Santa Fe as the site to do research on a secret military project.

At Los Alamos, scientists developed the world's first atomic bomb, a highly destructive nuclear weapon. It was first tested near Alamogordo, New Mexico, on July 16, 1945. People throughout the state noticed the flash and blast of

The world's first atomic-bomb explosion created a mushroom cloud that sprouted 40,000 feet (12,192 m).

the bomb, but few knew what had really happened. Some said the sun came up twice that day.

During the following month, the United States dropped two atomic bombs on Japan, bringing World War II to an end. In the years following the war, government projects at various laboratories in New Mexico have employed many New Mexicans. In addition to testing nuclear weapons, researchers at these labs work on projects such as finding better ways to use the sun's energy.

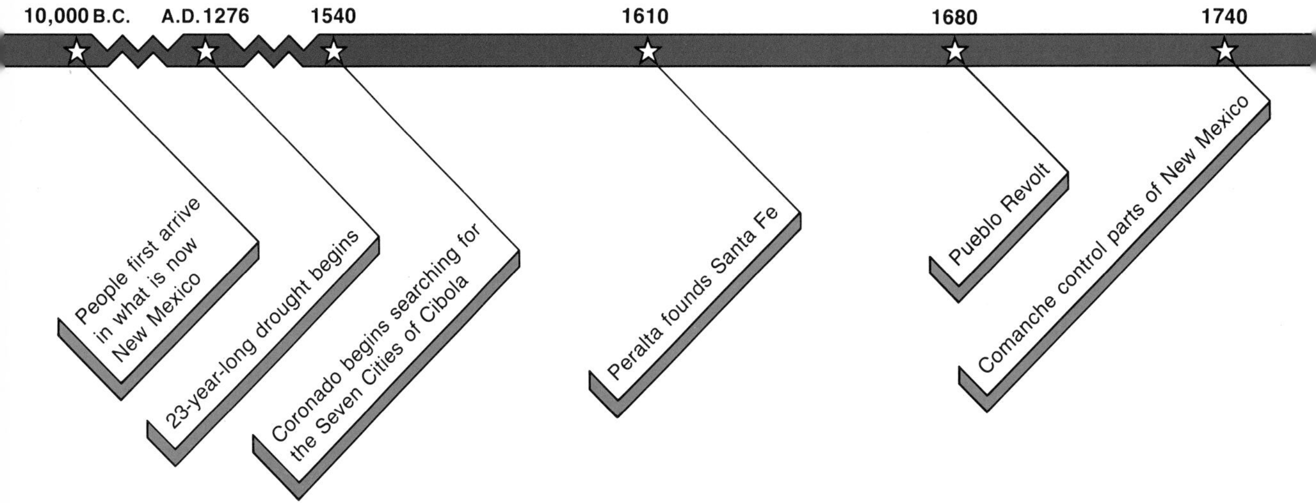

| 10,000 B.C. | A.D.1276 | 1540 | 1610 | 1680 | 1740 |

People first arrive in what is now New Mexico

23-year-long drought begins

Coronado begins searching for the Seven Cities of Cibola

Peralta founds Santa Fe

Pueblo Revolt

Comanche control parts of New Mexico

Along with modern scientific research, New Mexicans still practice age-old traditions. Spanish is one of the two official languages of the state government. Native American ceremonies take place regularly, and pottery is made the way it was hundreds of years ago. New Mexico's history and cultures still flavor daily life.

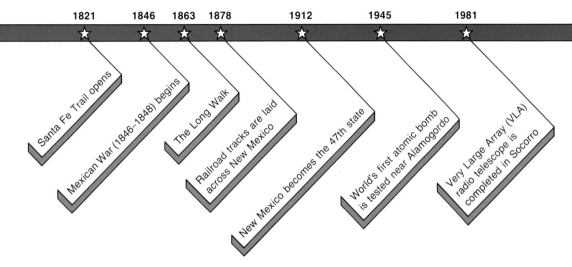

1821   1846   1863   1878   1912   1945   1981

Santa Fe Trail opens

Mexican War (1846–1848) begins

The Long Walk

Railroad tracks are laid across New Mexico

New Mexico becomes the 47th state

World's first atomic bomb is tested near Alamogordo

Very Large Array (VLA) radio telescope is completed in Socorro

The Very Large Array (VLA) radio telescope in Socorro, New Mexico, collects information about outer space by taking detailed photographs of the stars and planets.

Albuquerque is home to nearly 400,000 New Mexicans.

Living and Working in New Mexico

New Mexico seems very different from other states in the country. The mix of Pueblo, Navajo, Apache, **Latino**, and Anglo cultures has given the state a flavor all its own.

The variety of people, art, scenery, and jobs has attracted many newcomers to New Mexico. In fact, New Mexico is one of the fastest growing states in the country. Many of the new residents flock to the state's three largest cities— Albuquerque, Las Cruces, and Santa Fe (the capital).

At a festival in Taos, young Latinos show off a piñata, a figure decorated with brightly colored paper and filled with candy.

Almost half of the 1.5 million New Mexicans claim Latin American or Native American ancestry, or both. One out of every eleven people is Native American—a larger percentage than in most other states. The state's many reservations are home to Navajo, Ute, Apache, and Pueblo peoples.

Most of the reservations are poor, but several of them earn money from their mineral-rich land. The Navajo allow oil wells and mines on their reservation. Some lumber companies pay the Apache for the right to cut down trees on reservation land. In addition, the Apache have built resorts that offer hunting, golfing, and fishing to tourists.

A Navajo woman weaves a wool rug on a loom. Navajo rugs are famous for their detailed patterns.

People from all over the world shop for art at the Indian Market in Santa Fe. Visitors also taste Indian fry bread *(inset).*

Anglos—people without Latin American or American Indian heritage—make up more than half of New Mexico's population. African Americans and Asian Americans together make up less than 3 percent of the state's population.

Each cultural group in New Mexico proudly displays its traditional artwork. Every day, Native Americans line the plaza in front of the Palace of the Governors in Santa Fe to sell jewelry, weavings, paintings, and pottery. The best of the Native American artwork is sold at the Indian Market, held every summer in Santa Fe.

45

The Spanish markets, also held each year in Santa Fe, offer crafts, such as religious wood carvings and hand-painted tiles. And since the 1920s, Taos and Santa Fe have been home to large groups of Anglo artists and writers. The Santa Fe Opera and Santa Fe Community Theater add to the state capital's reputation as a fine-arts center.

Among the state's many historical and fine-arts museums are the Museum of New Mexico in Santa Fe and the Indian Pueblo Cultural Center in Albuquerque. The National Atomic Museum in Albuquerque and the Bradbury Science Museum in Los Alamos provide a history of nuclear research.

Latinos light hundreds of luminarias—candles placed in sand-filled bags—during holidays such as Christmas and Easter.

The International Balloon Fiesta attracts thousands of visitors to Albuquerque.

The International Balloon Fiesta, held every October in Albuquerque, has been called the most photographed event in the world. Hundreds of hot-air balloons fill the air at this colorful display. The New Mexico State Fair in Albuquerque includes a rodeo that is the largest in the world. Gallup hosts the Inter-Tribal Indian Ceremonial each year. At this event, 50 tribes from the United States and Mexico gather for a rodeo, dances, parades, and an art show.

47

Sports fans can watch horse racing at tracks in Albuquerque, La Mesa, Ruidoso, and Santa Fe. Crowds cheer on the University of New Mexico's basketball and football teams. And the Albuquerque Dukes, a minor-league team of the Los Angeles Dodgers, are a favorite of New Mexico's baseball fans.

New Mexico offers athletes and nature lovers a wide variety of activities. Hiking, horseback riding, fishing, white-water rafting, and skiing keep New Mexicans and visitors busy outdoors year-round.

New Mexico's outdoor activities attract thousands of tourists to the state each year. People who work serving the tourists and other people have service jobs. Eighty-one percent of New Mexico's work

Young New Mexicans celebrate the Fourth of July with sparklers.

force has some type of service job. Service workers include salesclerks, ski instructors, and government workers.

Paddling a kayak, a boater challenges the Rio Grande's rough waters.

Skiers glide down a slope near Santa Fe.

The campgrounds and trails of New Mexico's national parks are kept up by service workers who are called park attendants.

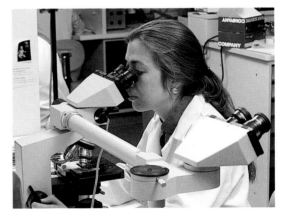

A scientist peers through her microscope at one of the state's research labs.

Most service workers in New Mexico work for the U.S. government. Some of these workers manage the state's national parks, forests, and grazing lands. Many people have jobs with the government's defense and energy departments. At Los Alamos National Laboratory, Sandia National Laboratories, and White Sands Missile Range, New Mexicans study nuclear energy or make and test nuclear weapons.

New Mexico has programs to prepare young people for high-technology jobs. The state's government labs and high-tech companies hire these trained workers. Some of the companies make weapons, computer parts, and electrical equipment. Other manufacturers in the state make food products, appliances, and wood products. Seven percent of New Mexico's workers are employed in manufacturing.

Military rockets point to the sky at Kirtland Air Force Base in Albuquerque.

Mining is another important industry in the state. In fact, New Mexico is a leading mining state, supplying the nation with oil, coal, natural gas, copper, and uranium —a mineral used in creating nuclear energy.

New Mexico's supply of oil is being used up as miners empty the oil fields in the state. But New Mexico still earns about 80 percent of its mining income from oil. Most of the state's oil comes from fields in the southeastern part of the state.

Rainfall is scarce in New Mexico, and much of the state's soil is poor. These two conditions make it impossible for many crops to

Hot, spicy chili peppers flavor many New Mexican foods, including pinto beans, corn tortillas, stews, and burritos.

Of the 1.4 million cows in New Mexico, 40 percent are beef cattle.

survive. Only about 3 percent of New Mexico's workers have jobs on farms and ranches.

Crops that do grow well in the state need to have water channeled to them from streams and rivers. This process, called **irrigation,** allows New Mexicans to harvest chili peppers, corn, cotton, hay, wheat, and apples. Most of New Mexico's agricultural products come from the Rio Grande Valley and the Great Plains region. Beef cattle, dairy cattle, and sheep graze on ranches throughout the state. In fact, with nearly two million farm animals, New Mexico has more livestock than people!

Protecting the Environment

J. Robert Oppenheimer

New Mexico's ties to nuclear science go back to the 1940s and to J. Robert Oppenheimer. The state's laboratories are still leaders in nuclear research, and now the state is also a leader in another important and related issue—where to store **nuclear waste.**

Nuclear waste is garbage tainted with **radiation.** The waste may include parts from nuclear bombs, fuel rods from nuclear power plants, or parts from hospital x-ray machines.

Because nuclear waste is **radioactive**, it is dangerous. Radiation gives off invisible rays and particles that can be harmful to humans. Too much radiation can kill living things. It can cause diseases and birth defects. Radiation is especially dangerous because it has no taste or smell. Some kinds of radiation can pass unnoticed through skin, walls, rock, and metal.

Nuclear waste gives off harmful radiation for a long time—even hundreds of thousands of years. If nuclear waste is so hazardous, why do we continue to produce it?

Nuclear energy and other sources of radiation do have some benefits. Nuclear power plants that produce electricity create less air pollution than other sources of electricity, such as coal. Some people feel that the threat of nuclear war is so terrifying that having nuclear weapons can prevent an enemy from starting a war. And X rays help doctors find their patients' ailments.

Nuclear power plants do not normally produce air pollution.

But these benefits leave the country with a problem. Where do we safely store nuclear waste? At one time, Los Alamos dumped nuclear waste in nearby canyons. Some of the waste eventually washed into local streams and rivers. Since then, an unusually large number of people who live downstream from Los Alamos have developed cancer.

Looking for solutions, the U.S. Department of Energy has chosen a spot in New Mexico where nuclear waste could be stored more safely. If opened, the Waste Isolation Pilot Plant (WIPP) near Carlsbad could be the first long-term storage site for low-level nuclear waste from around the country. Low-level nuclear waste includes contaminated gloves and tools used by workers in nuclear power plants and in nuclear weapons laboratories.

Low-level nuclear waste—including rags, rubber gloves, lab coats, and tools exposed to radioactivity—is sealed in airtight buckets.

Waste Isolation Pilot Plant (WIPP)

With an environmental researcher from WIPP, students from the Carlsbad area test soil for radioactivity.

The WIPP site is a series of caves dug thousands of feet under the earth in beds of salt. The caves have been prepared to hold containers of nuclear waste, but people are still arguing about whether WIPP should ever be used.

Many New Mexicans approve of WIPP. Some of them work at nuclear laboratories or know people who do. They know that people are working to improve storage systems for nuclear waste. They trust that the government knows how to handle nuclear waste safely. WIPP also employs many people in New Mexico, bringing lots of money to the state. And people realize that the country has already produced tons of low-level nuclear waste and that every day it produces more. The waste has to be put somewhere.

Other people are fighting to stop WIPP. They don't believe that the site will be safe. Over time, nuclear waste changes. It gives off dangerous gases, and it can become very hot, eventually causing the salt in the caves to ooze and crush the containers. Some people fear that the damaged containers would leak radiation, which would then enter New Mexico's underground water supplies.

Elementary students in New Mexico have been sending long letters asking the government to stop using nuclear power.

Tens of thousands of truckloads of low-level nuclear waste from around the country are already scheduled to be taken to WIPP. Low-level waste from Los Alamos and other places would be trucked right through crowded neighborhoods in Santa Fe. If a truck carrying nuclear waste were in a highway accident, the waste could leak, endangering entire communities. Would it be safer to store the waste closer to where it was created?

Future accidents are another concern. What if someone unknow-

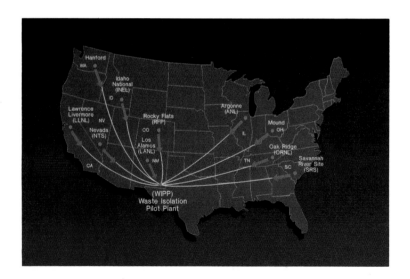

Plans allow for low-level nuclear waste to be shipped to WIPP from several states.

ingly drills into WIPP 10,000 years from now? How can the government protect people from the waste for that long?

Even those who support WIPP agree that it's not a total solution. Every day, hospitals, nuclear laboratories, and nuclear power plants across the country produce more waste. WIPP only has room for the low-level waste we've already produced. And it will probably take 25 years to carry all that waste to WIPP. What will we do with the waste we produce in the next 25 years?

Protesters demand that WIPP be stopped.

New Mexico's Famous People

Bruce Cabot (1904–1972) played the hero who saved Fay Wray from the oversize gorilla in the 1933 film *King Kong*. Cabot was born in Carlsbad, New Mexico.

Demi Moore (born 1962) is an actress from Roswell, New Mexico. Moore began her television career on the daytime soap opera "General Hospital." She has since starred in several movies, including *St. Elmo's Fire* and *Ghost*.

BRUCE CABOT *(right)* ▲

DEMI MOORE ▶

MARÍA MONTOYA ▲
MARTÍNEZ

GEORGIA O'KEEFE ▶

ARTISTS

Pablita Velarde (born 1918), a painter from Santa Clara Pueblo, New Mexico, is one of the most famous Native American painters in the world. In her work, she applies painting techniques and styles from her Tewa Indian heritage.

María Montoya Martínez (1887–1980) encouraged Native American artists to practice the arts of their ancestors. Martínez, a Pueblo Indian, was a potter from San Ildefonso Pueblo, New Mexico. She was known for her black-on-black pottery.

Georgia O'Keeffe (1887–1986), a painter, spent a lot of time visiting New Mexico before finally moving to a house near Abiquiu in 1950. Many of her paintings feature the wildflowers, sand dunes, and animal skulls of the state's deserts.

BUSINESS LEADER & POLITICIANS

Conrad Hilton (1887–1979) formed the Hilton Hotel Corporation in 1946. The company now runs hotels and restaurants throughout the United States. Hilton was born in San Antonio, New Mexico.

Chee Dodge (1860–1947), from Crystal, New Mexico, founded and chaired the Navajo Tribal Council, the first official government of the Navajo Indians. He led the council from 1923 through the 1930s, helping the tribe work with the U.S. government.

Joseph Montoya (1915–1978) was elected to the New Mexico House of Representatives when he was only 21 years old. In 1965 he became the first Latino politician to be elected to the U.S. Senate. Montoya was born in Peña Blanca, New Mexico.

◀ CONRAD HILTON

JOSEPH MONTOYA ▶

▲ WILLIAM HANNA *(left)*

CARTOONISTS

William Hanna (born 1910), with his partner Joseph Barbera, created many popular cartoons for television. "Yogi Bear," "Tom and Jerry," "Jetsons," and "The Flintstones" are just a few of the cartoons that Hanna-Barbera Productions has made. Hanna was born in Melrose, New Mexico.

Bill Mauldin (born 1921) won the Pulitzer Prize in 1945 and again in 1959 for his cartoons of U.S. Army GIs, or soldiers, Willie and Joe. His characters first appeared during World War II in *Stars and Stripes*, the U.S. Army newspaper, and later became popular throughout the country. Mauldin is from Mountain Park, New Mexico.

63

EXPLORERS

Florence Hawley Ellis (1917–1991) taught anthropology, or the study of human culture, at the University of New Mexico. Ellis also led important archaeological digs at sites near Santa Fe and in the Chaco Canyon.

Harrison Schmitt (born 1935), of Santa Rita, New Mexico, piloted the *Apollo 17* lunar module—a spacecraft used for traveling to the moon—in 1972. From 1977 to 1983, the former astronaut served as a U.S. senator from New Mexico.

▲ HARRISON SCHMITT

◄ JOHN DENVER

MUSICIAN & DANCER

John Denver (born 1943) is a singer and songwriter. "Take Me Home Country Road" and "Rocky Mountain High" are two of his well-known country songs. Denver was born in Roswell, New Mexico.

Amanda McKerrow (born 1964) is a ballerina from Albuquerque. In 1981 she won the gold medal at the Moscow International Ballet Competition. McKerrow is a principal dancer with the American Ballet Theatre.

REBEL & HERO

William H. Bonney (1859?–1881), better known as Billy the Kid, moved from New York to Silver City, New Mexico, in 1868. He soon became feared as a cattle thief and gunfighter. Bonney managed to escape from jail several times.

Popé (1630?–1692), from San Juan Pueblo, was an American Indian religious leader who drove the Spaniards out of New

WILLIAM BONNEY ▶

64

Mexico in 1680. He then restored religious freedom throughout the Pueblo communities.

SPORTS FIGURES

Ralph Kiner (born 1922), of Santa Rita, New Mexico, played baseball from 1946 to 1955, mainly with the Pittsburgh Pirates. For seven straight seasons, Kiner hit more home runs than any other player in the National League. Kiner later became a sportscaster.

Al Unser (born 1939) and **Bobby Unser** (born 1924) are two of the country's most famous race-car drivers. The brothers were born and raised in Albuquerque in a large family of racers and have won seven Indianapolis 500 races.

▲ BOBBY UNSER

WRITERS

Mary Austin (1868–1934) settled in Santa Fe in 1924. Her house became a meeting place for many important writers in the area. Austin's books, which describe the lives of Indians in the Southwest, include *The Land of Little Rain* and *Isidro*.

MARY ▶
AUSTIN

Mark Medoff (born 1940) is a playwright and a professor of drama at the University of New Mexico. One of Medoff's plays, *Children of a Lesser God,* was performed on Broadway before being made into an award-winning motion picture in 1986.

John Nichols (born 1940) has written several novels. While living near Taos, Nichols wrote a set of stories that take place in northern New Mexico—*The Milagro Beanfield War, The Magic Journey,* and *The Nirvana Blues.*

65

Facts-at-a-Glance

Nickname: Land of Enchantment
Song: "O, Fair New Mexico"
Motto: *Crescit Eundo*
  (It Grows as It Goes)
Flower: yucca flower
Tree: piñon
Bird: roadrunner

Population: 1,515,069*
Rank in population, nationwide: 37th
Area: 121,598 sq mi (314,929 sq km)
Rank in area, nationwide: 5th
Date and ranking of statehood:
  January 6, 1912, the 47th state
Capital: Santa Fe
Major cities (and populations*): Albuquerque
  (384,736), Las Cruces (62,126), Santa Fe
  (55,859), Roswell (44,654), Farmington
  (33,997)
U.S. senators: 2
U.S. representatives: 3
Electoral votes: 5

Places to visit: Museum of New Mexico in Santa Fe, Mission of San Miguel in Santa Fe, Taos Pueblo in Taos, Lea County Cowboy Hall of Fame and Western Heritage Center in Hobbs, Billy the Kid Museum in Fort Sumner

Annual events: Winterfest in Santa Fe (Feb.), Dinosaur Days in Clayton (April), Inter-Tribal Indian Ceremonial in Gallup (Aug.), International Balloon Fiesta in Albuquerque (Oct.), Old-Time Fiddlers Contest in Truth or Consequences (Oct.), Luminaria Bus Tours in Albuquerque (Dec.)

*1990 census

| **Average January temperature:** 34° F (1° C) | **Average July temperature:** 74° F (23° C) |

Natural resources: forests, coal, natural gas, petroleum, silver, gold, copper, uranium, potash, helium gas

Agricultural products: beef cattle, milk, hay, chili peppers, pecans, cotton

Manufactured goods: computer parts, appliances, communication systems, petroleum products, nuclear products

ENDANGERED SPECIES
Mammals—Mexican long-nosed bat, Peñasco least chipmunk, gray wolf, desert bighorn sheep
Birds—brown pelican, peregrine falcon, whooping crane, piping plover, common ground-dove, thick-billed kingbird
Reptiles—Gila monster, bunch grass lizard, gray-checkered whiptail, Mexican garter snake
Fish—Gila trout, spikedace, bluntnose shiner
Plants—gypsum wild buckwheat, Knowlton cactus, McKittrick pennyroyal, Pecos sunflower

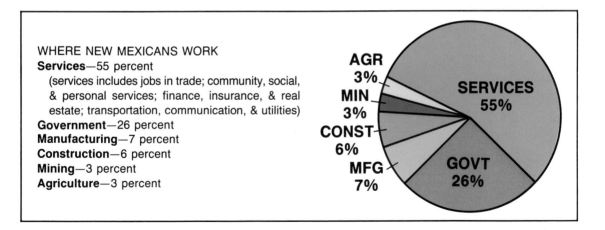

WHERE NEW MEXICANS WORK
Services—55 percent
　(services includes jobs in trade; community, social, & personal services; finance, insurance, & real estate; transportation, communication, & utilities)
Government—26 percent
Manufacturing—7 percent
Construction—6 percent
Mining—3 percent
Agriculture—3 percent

AGR
3%
MIN
3%
CONST
6%
MFG
7%
SERVICES
55%
GOVT
26%

PRONUNCIATION GUIDE

Alamogordo (al-uh-muh-GAWRD-oh)

Albuquerque (AL-buh-kuhr-kee)

Anasazi (ahn-uh-SAHZ-ee)

Apache (uh-PACH-ee)

Comanche (kuh-MAN-chee)

Gila (HEE-luh)

Las Cruces (lahs KROO-sehs)

Los Alamos (lohs AL-uh-mohs)

Navajo (NAV-uh-hoh)

Pueblo (poo-EHB-loh)

Rio Grande (ree-oh GRAND) or (ree-oh GRAHN-day)

San Juan (san WAHN)

Santa Fe (sant-uh FAY)

Taos (TAUS)

Glossary

Anglo   Historically, a white person who lives in the United States. Anglo is a term used primarily in the Southwest and has come to include African Americans and Asian Americans.

basin   A bowl-shaped region. Also, all the land drained by a river and its branches.

colony   A territory ruled by a country some distance away.

desert   An area of land that receives only about 10 inches (25 cm) or less of rain or snow a year. Some deserts are mountainous; others are expanses of rock, sand, or salt flats.

drought   A long period of extreme dryness due to lack of rain or snow.

Dust Bowl   An area of the Great Plains region that suffered from long dry spells and severe dust storms, especially during the 1930s.

irrigation A method of watering land by directing water through canals, ditches, pipes, or sprinklers.

Latino A person living in the United States who either came from or has ancestors from Latin America. Latin America includes Mexico and much of Central and South America.

lava Hot, melted rock that erupts from a volcano or from cracks in the earth's surface and that hardens as it cools.

mesa An isolated hill with steep sides and a flat top.

nuclear waste Waste that gives off dangerous rays of energy and particles called radiation.

plateau A large, relatively flat area that stands above the surrounding land.

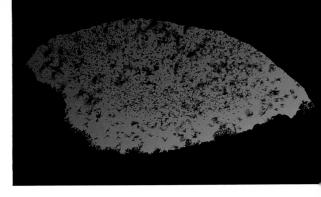

Carlsbad Caverns

radiation Often harmful rays of energy and particles given off when atoms and molecules change to other elements.

radioactive Giving off rays of energy called radiation when the atoms of certain elements change to other elements.

reservation Public land set aside by the government to be used by Native Americans.

treaty An agreement between two or more groups, usually having to do with peace or trade.

Index

70

Acknowledgments:

Maryland Cartographics, Inc., pp. 2, 10; Betty Groskin, pp. 2–3, 47; Harold Walter, p. 6; Toby Schnobrich, p. 7; R. E. Barber, © 1993, pp. 8 (left), 17 (top), 18, 44; Kent & Donna Dannen, pp. 8–9, 13, 14, 20, 22, 45 (inset), 49 (top), 51; Charles S. Swenson, pp. 11, 12, 17 (bottom); © James Blank/Root Resources, pp. 15, 42; Frederica Georgia, pp. 16, 25, 45 (bottom), 48, 69; Library of Congress, pp. 21, 29, 54; Tony La Gruth, p. 23; The Southwest Museum, Los Angeles, Photo #CT.551, p. 24; Edward E. Ayer Collection, The Newberry Library, Chicago, p. 26; Museum of New Mexico, pp. 28 (Neg. No. 6977), 31 (Neg. No. 152188), 33 (Edward S. Curtis, Neg. No. 143874), 34–5 (Ben Wittick, School of American Research Collections, Neg. No. 15870), 36 (Neg. No. 92018), 62 (bottom left, Wyatt Davis, Neg. No. 4591), 62 (bottom right, Neg. No. 9763); New Mexico State Records Center and Archives, pp. 32 (F. McNitt Collection, #5702), 35 (top right, D. Woodward Collection, #22697), 38 (R. V. Hunter Collection, #23057); Center for Southwest Research, Gen. Library, Univ. of New Mexico, pp. 35 (bottom right, Henry A. Schmidt, Neg. No. 000–179–0736), 65 (bottom, Neg. No. 000–255–0461); U.S. Army, p. 39; © Stan Osolinski/Root Resources, p. 41; Ray Lutz, Taos County Chamber of Commerce, p. 43; Ron Behrmann, Albuquerque Convention & Visitors Bureau, p. 46; Mark Nohl, New Mexico Economic & Tourism Dept. pp. 49 (bottom), 50 (right); Theresa Early, pp. 50 (left), 71; Jack Parsons, p. 52; © D. Newman/Visuals Unlimited, p. 53; Jerry Miller, Northern States Power Co., p. 55; U.S. Dept. of Energy, pp. 56, 57, 58, 60; Michel Monteaux, pp. 59, 61; Wisconsin Center for Film and Theater Research, p. 62 (top left); Hollywood Book & Poster Co., p. 62 (top right); Hilton Hotels Corp., p. 63 (top left); Independent Picture Service, pp. 63 (top right), 64 (bottom right); Cleveland Public Library, pp. 63 (bottom), 65 (top left); NASA, p. 64 (top); RCA, p. 64 (bottom left); Indianapolis Motor Speedway, p. 65 (top right); Jean Matheny, p. 66.